P9-BYN-273

For Dr. Michael Droller W.S.
For Monique T.E.

Text copyright © 2001 by William Steig/Pictures copyright © 2001 by Teryl Euvremer

All rights reserved/Library of Congress catalog card number: 99-65173

Printed in the United States of America/Designed by Atha Tehon/First edition, 2001

Joanna Cotler Books

An Imprint of HarperCollins*Publishers*

Toby, What Are You?

Story by **WILLIAM STEIG**

Pictures by **TERYL EUVREMER**

Arriving home one day, Toby's father is surprised
to see his son lying facedown by the door.

"I wonder what I'll be in my dream,"
Toby mumbles as he falls asleep.

Toby gets tucked in, with four or five loud good-night kisses.

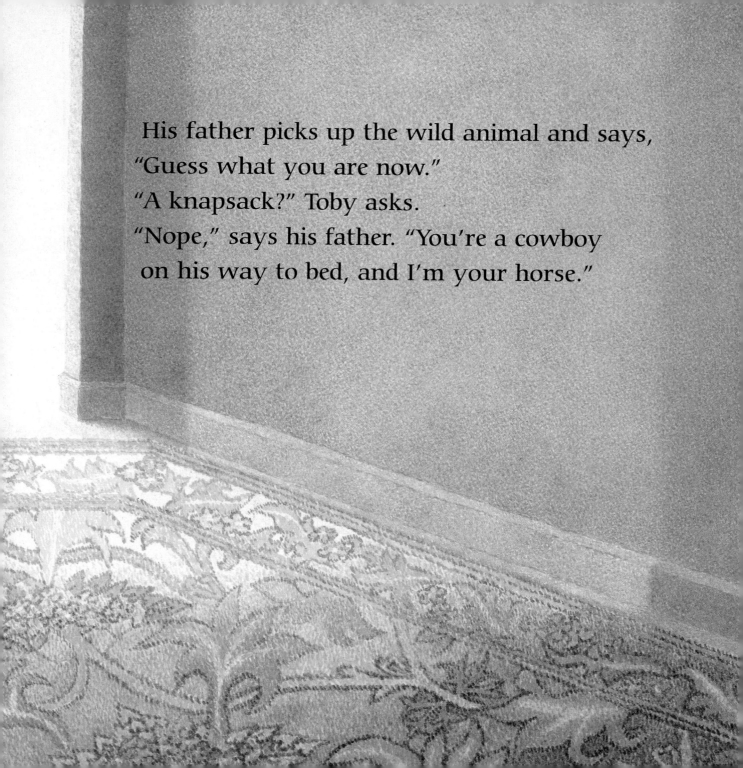

His father picks up the wild animal and says,
"Guess what you are now."
"A knapsack?" Toby asks.
"Nope," says his father. "You're a cowboy
on his way to bed, and I'm your horse."

Now it's bedtime, but something scary turns up, growling.

"Oh, no!" Toby's mother hollers.

"A dangerous wild animal!"

"Guess this one, if you can," says Toby.
"Will you go to bed if we get it?" asks his mother.
"Okay," Toby answers.
"Let's see—you're a
 wobbly coffee table!"
"I am," says Toby.

At dinner, Toby's parents are stumped.
"Give up?"says Toby.
"I'm a mountain . . . with snow on top!"
"Oh?" say the two parents.

"I see a fish trapped in a net," says his father.
"Wrong, wrong, and triple wrong," says Toby.
"I'm a plate of spaghetti."

Toby comes into the kitchen, saying,
"Here's a hard one!"
"Well," says his mother,
"you're in a chicken coop, so you're a chicken."
"No, no, no," says Toby. "I'm a flyswatter."

In another little while, Toby yells, "You'll never get this one!"

"You must be a sandwich," says his mother.

"Yes, but what kind?" says Toby.

"A banana sandwich, of course!"

"Right," says Toby.

Then they hear a muffled voice calling, "What now?"
"That's easy," says his father. "You're a turnip."
"Wrong again," says the voice.
"I'm a bag of dirty laundry!"

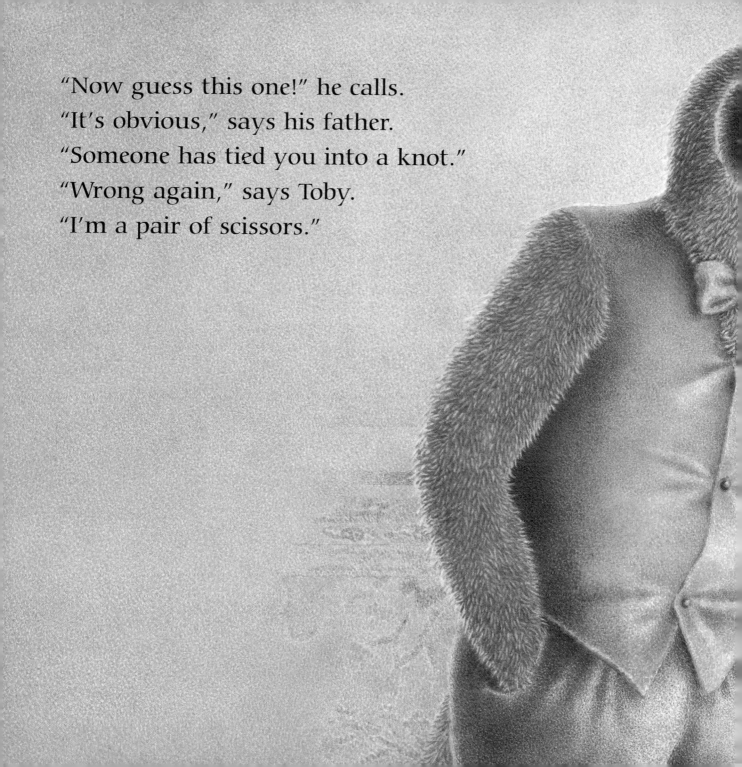

"Now guess this one!" he calls.
"It's obvious," says his father.
"Someone has tied you into a knot."
"Wrong again," says Toby.
"I'm a pair of scissors."

Then Toby says, "What am I now?"
His mother looks and says, "Definitely a camel."
"Wrong!" says Toby. "Don't you know a bridge when you see one? There's even a boat in the water."

A little bit later, Toby's parents hear him ask,
"*Now* what do you think I am?"
"A clothes tree!" they both exclaim.
"Correct!" says Toby.

"Guess what I am," says Toby.
  His father thinks for a moment and cries,
"Aha, a new doormat."
  He carefully pretends to wipe his feet
  on his son and goes in.